Hamsters
to the Rescue

Ellen Stoll Walsh

Harcourt, Inc
Orlando Austin New York San Diego Toronto London

www.HarcourtBooks.com

Library of Congress Cataloging-in-Publication Data
Walsh, Ellen Stoll.
Hamsters to the rescue/Ellen Stoll Walsh.
p. cm.
Summary: When two hamsters find a feather on the beach, they set out to find the
seagull that lost it, meeting new friends and overcoming obstacles as they go.
[1. Hamsters—Fiction. 2. Feathers—Fiction. 3. Lost and found possessions—Fiction.
4. Crabs—Fiction. 5. Gulls—Fiction. 6. Beaches—Fiction.] I. Title.
PZ7.W1675Ham 2005
[E]—dc22 2004021027
ISBN 0-15-205202-X

First edition
A C E G H F D B

Manufactured in China

The illustrations in this book are cut-paper collage.
The text type was set in OPTI Berling.
Color separations by Bright Arts Ltd., Hong Kong
Manufactured by SNP Leefung Holdings Limited, China
This book was printed on totally chlorine-free Stora Enso Matte paper.
Production supervision by Ginger Boyer
Designed by Barry Age

For Jane and Stoney

One day while the hamsters were visiting the beach, Henry found a feather.

"I wonder where it came from?" said Pell.

"I think the seagull lost it," said Henry.

Pell looked at the sky. "He's not up there. Maybe he needs the feather to help him fly."

"We'd better search for him and give it back," said Henry. "Let's look in the sand dunes."

Hamster feet sank deep in the soft, dry sand as Henry and Pell climbed up and down, up and down.

"I don't see the seagull," said Pell.

"Maybe the sand swallowed him," said Henry. "It sure is trying to swallow *me*."

"How's the feather?" asked Pell.

"Sandy," said Henry.

They came to some rocks. "Watch me take the feather down the slide!" said Henry.

"Be careful with it," Pell said, and she slid down the rock after him.

"Look, Pell," said Henry as he reached the bottom. "A seashell is running down the beach."

The hamsters ran after it. "Caught it!" said Pell.

"This is my shell," said the hermit crab inside. "I live here."

"Sorry," said Henry. "We're looking for the seagull. We think he lost this feather."

"Have you seen him?" said Pell.

"I try *not* to see him," said the hermit crab.

"Seagulls eat hermit crabs." And he scuttled off.

Henry found a shell nearby and climbed in. "Look, Pell, I'm a hermit crab," he said.

"Careful," said Pell. "The seagull might eat you. I just hope seagulls don't eat hamsters, too."

"Not if we're nice enough to bring back his feather!" said Henry. "Let's try the tide pool."

On the way, the wind snatched the feather and sent it dancing and skipping over the sand. The hamsters danced and skipped after it...

… until—just like that—it disappeared.

"Oh no," said Henry. "Now we have to find the feather before we find the seagull."

"Let's keep going," said Pell. "Maybe we'll catch up to it at the tide pool."

But all they found there was a fiddler crab. He was stirring plankton. "Care to join me for lunch?" he said.

"No thanks," said Pell.

"Hey," said Henry, "that stirring thing looks familiar."

"It's our feather!" cried Pell.

"Sorry," said the fiddler crab. "But it did come in handy."

"The feather looks terrible now," said Henry. "What will the seagull think?"

"Let's try to fix it," said Pell. They each gave a tug.

Snap!

"Uh-oh," said Henry. "Now what will we do?"

"Look, Henry!" said Pell. "There's no time to fix the feather now. I think these are seagull footprints."

"There are footprints on the footprints," said Henry. "They're all mixed up. The seagull was probably looking for his feather."

"They haven't been here long," said Pell, "or the tide would have washed them away."

"Do you think we're getting close?" said Henry.

"Closer and closer," said Pell.

"Where are you, seagull?" shouted Henry.

"Look, I see him!" whispered Pell. "I think he heard you, because here he comes."

"At last," said Henry. "But I didn't know he would be so big."

"He's bigger than big," said Pell. "Do you still think he won't eat hamsters?"

"Not if we have his feather," said Henry.

"We broke it," said Pell. "It looks terrible."

"Maybe we should run," said Henry.

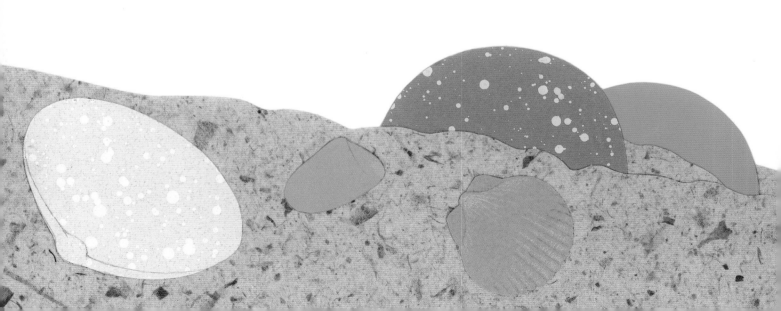

But the seagull was already there. "Wait," he said.
"Were you looking for me?"

The hamsters gave him the feather. "Sorry," said Henry. "We found it for you, but it got messed up."

"And we don't taste good," added Pell.

The seagull laughed a deep-down rumbly laugh. "Don't worry," he said. "I'm not going to eat you. And I grow new feathers when old ones fall out. But thank you for bringing my feather to me. Your kindness makes me happy."

"You're welcome," said Henry and Pell.

"Here are some more feathers just the right size for hamsters," said the seagull.

"Now we can be seagulls, too!" said Pell.

"I'm flying," said Henry, flapping hard.

"Henry, you dropped a feather," said Pell.

"That's okay," said Henry. "I'll grow a new one."

When all of their feathers had fallen out, Pell said,
"We're hamsters again."

"What can we find now?" said Henry.

"It's getting late," said Pell. "Let's find our way home."

Can you find these shells
in Henry and Pell's story?

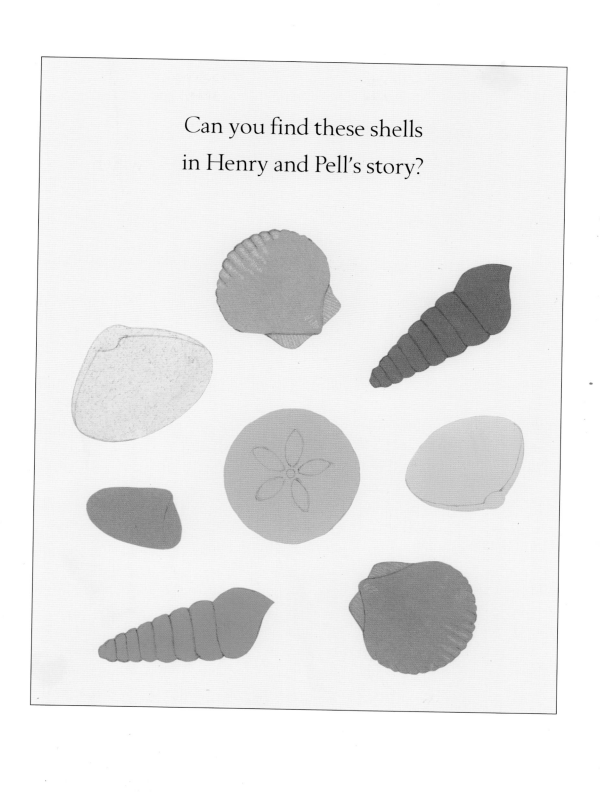